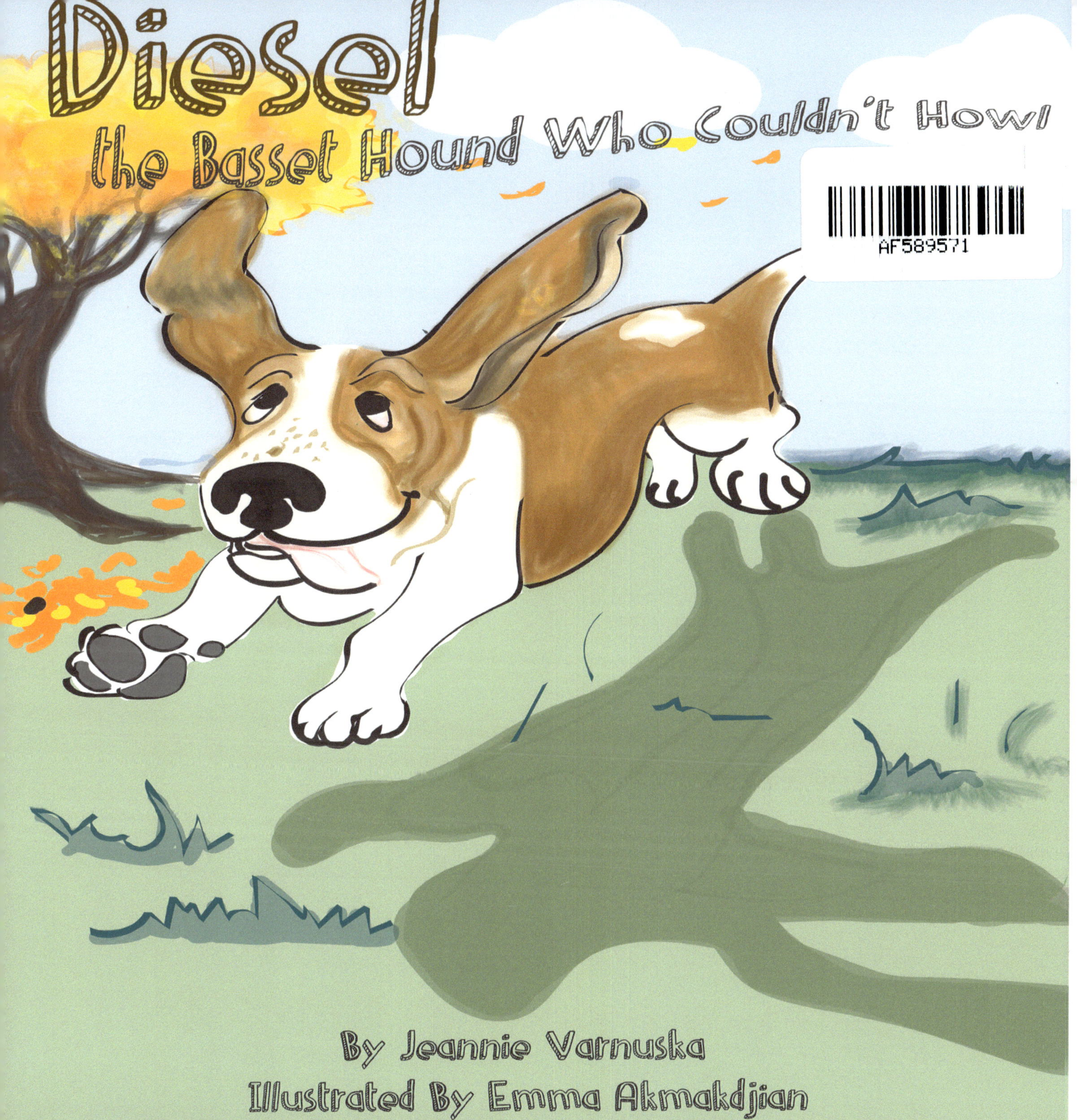
Diesel
the Basset Hound Who Couldn't Howl
By Jeannie Varnuska
Illustrated By Emma Akmakdjian

ISBN: 979-8-89228-126-3 (Paperback)
ISBN: 979-8-89228-127-0 (Hardcover)
ISBN: 979-8-89228-128-7 (eBook)

Printed in the United States of America

Diesel is a basset hound
who has three brothers and two sisters.

Basset hounds are short, and

I mean REALLY, **REALLY**, **REALLY** short.

Basset hounds have the longest ears of any dog.

Since Diesel is so short, and his ears are so long
he trips on them when he runs.

Tumbling over and over.

It's kind of like when your shoelaces are untied.

Poor Diesel his long ears would get dirty
dragging on the ground when he walked.

When he ate his ears would end up in his food bowl. When he drank his ears would get soooo wet he would have to shake his head again and again to try to get them dry.

On really windy days Diesel has to be really careful
because his ears make a great kite.

Can you imagine a flying basset hound?

However, with all these little problems Diesel was still a happy go lucky little basset.

He liked playing ball, sleeping with his sock monkey, and rough housing with his brothers and sisters.

Until one day his brother Tommy decided to howl.

This is what basset hounds do.

"ARRRRROOOOOOOOOOOO" Tommy howled.

This first howl from Tommy is what was the beginning of Diesel's worst problem ever.

All at once all of Diesels brothers and sisters began howling.

"ARRRROOOO, ARRRRROOOO", each and every brother and sister howled and howled all except for Diesel.

His brothers and sisters stopped howling and looked at Diesel waiting for his howl.

"ARF" Diesel said in a soft voice. Then his brothers and sisters did a very mean thing.

They laughed and laughed at Diesel.

All except for sister Susie, who said "Come on Diesel, try again you can do this. I know you can!"

Diesel looked at sister Susie took a very deep breath and said "ARF."

The laughter continued but this time it was louder.

Diesel's brother Fred said "no one wants a basset hound who can't howl, you'll never get a family."

This made Diesel sadder and more determined to howl.

Poor Diesel he went into the backyard to the very back by the old oak tree and tried and tried to howl.

Yet, all that came out was "ARF."

Diesel worried about not getting a family until he fell asleep.

The next morning a woman came and took Sister Susie to her new home.

A few hours later more people and families came and took all Diesels brothers and sisters to their new homes.

Diesel knew that brother Fred had been right, since he couldn't howl he would never have a family to love him.

With no one to play with, Diesel laid on his bed with a very unhappy, long, sad face, even his sock monkey couldn't cheer him up.

Days, weeks, maybe even months went by for Diesel is not very good at telling time, when a lady came and wanted a basset hound.

Diesel liked her immediately, she had hair golden like the sun.

Since all his brothers and sisters were gone he secretly hoped he would finally have a new home.

"Well he's the only one left and he doesn't howl." Said Diesel's keeper.

"Really? I thought all basset hounds howled." Replied the golden haired lady.

Diesel was nervous and worried, he needed to impress the lady with the golden hair.

He needed to howl so she would give him a family to love. He took a DEEP breath and decided he could and would howl.

Then with all his might he opened his mouth "ARF" was what came out.

His heart sank, he would never get a family. The one chance he had and he just couldn't howl.

However, the lady with the golden hair smiled, then laughed, scooped Diesel up and said "He's perfect."

DOG
TREATS

Diesel loved the lady with the golden hair and she loved him.

They took long walks, played ball and Diesel learned many new tricks.

He could sit, stay, beg, shake and give a high five with his paw.

Diesel secretly practiced his howling but knew the lady with the golden hair loved him no matter what.

One day Diesel and the lady with the golden hair went to a place called the library.

There were lots and lots of books and children who wanted to read to Diesel.

Diesel sat quietly listening to the different stories that were read to him.

He loved the attention, the stories, and the children who stroked and petted him.

When it was time to go the lady with the golden hair hugged Diesel very tight, then whispered in his ear.

"You can't howl and that's okay because you are so good at helping kids like reading, and making people happy that's so much more important than howling."

No one is good at everything, but EVERYONE is good at something.

Diesel's heart was so happy, he looked up at the lady with golden hair and said "ARF!"

www.ingramcontent.com/pod-product-compliance
Ingram Content Group UK Ltd.
Pitfield, Milton Keynes, MK11 3LW, UK
UKHW061027310726
14090UKWH00026B/185
* 9 7 9 8 8 9 2 2 8 1 2 6 3 *